D1124090

The Fantastic Drawings of DANIELLE

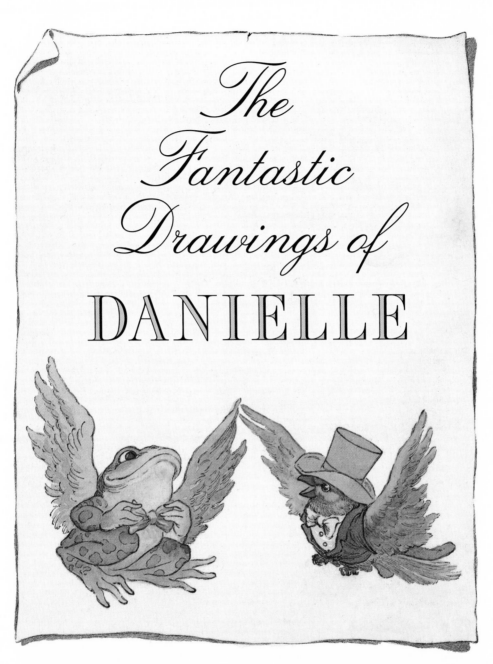

BARBARA McCLINTOCK

Houghton Mifflin Company Boston 1996

Copyright © 1996 by Barbara McClintock

All rights reserved. For information about permission
to reproduce selections from this book, write to
Permissions, Houghton Mifflin Company, 215 Park Avenue South,
New York, New York 10003.

For information about this and other Houghton Mifflin
trade and reference books and multimedia products,
visit The Bookstore at Houghton Mifflin on the World Wide
Web at http://www.hmco.com/trade/.

Manufactured in the United States of America

Book design by David Saylor
The text of this book is set in 16-point Monotype Baskerville.
The artwork is watercolor, sepia ink, and gouache,
reproduced in full color.

HOR   10   9   8   7   6   5   4   3   2   1

Library of Congress Cataloging-in-Publication Data
McClintock, Barbara
The fantastic drawings of Danielle / Barbara McClintock.
p.   cm.
Summary: Even though her photographer father urges her
to try a more practical form of art, a young artist in turn-of-
the-century Paris finds that her talent for drawing can be useful.
ISBN 0-395-73980-2
[1. Artists—Fiction. 2. Fathers and daughters—Fiction.]
I. Title.   PZ7. M47841418Fan 1996   [Fic]—dc20
94-48842   CIP   AC

♻ Interior pages and dust jacket printed on recycled paper.

To
my
parents

$\mathcal{D}$ANIELLE loved to draw. She drew odd and wonderful things, dancing storks and dashing foxes—the more fantastic, the better. She drew constantly.

Her father was a photographer, and he didn't understand her drawings at all. "Flying frogs! Birds in top hats! You should draw what's real or use the camera."

Even though Danielle knew her father loved her, she secretly wished she could make him proud of her, too.

One morning Danielle decided to draw exactly what her father photographed.

The result wasn't what she had planned.

That evening, she tried again.

"It just looks like a flower. Boring."

"Maybe if I do this and . . ."

"Papa! I can't help it." Suddenly Danielle didn't feel like much of an artist.

Once a week Papa sold his photographs.
"Nothing today. Maybe next week."

"None of these, thanks."

"Let's go inside where it's warm."
They ordered pastries and tried to be cheerful.

"Look, Papa. A goat! He wants to buy all your pictures
for his collection."

Papa smiled. "He's a goat with good taste, then."

In silence they walked home.

The next morning Danielle's father was sick with a high fever.

Danielle took care of him every day.

She spent their small hoard of money as carefully as she could.

And every night she drew.

After only one week, their money ran out.

Danielle didn't know what to do.
Fear grew to panic.
If only there were photographs to sell.

"I'll have to take some new photographs myself."
Carefully she packed her father's equipment.

"It can't be that hard to use a camera." Danielle's footsteps echoed as she clattered down the empty staircase.

The morning was white and cold, but Danielle walked
firmly through the softly falling snow.

"Time to set up the camera.
Let's see, first the legs."

"Now the plate. I think it goes
this way, or maybe like this."

"That's not right either. It looks
so easy when Papa does it."

"Hey, look out!"

"Papa's camera! Almost broken!"

"This is impossible."

A woman paused nearby. "Aren't you the photographer's daughter?"
Miserable as she was, Danielle offered a polite yes.

"I'm Camille Beton, a painter. Sometimes I buy pictures from your
father. What are you doing out here in the snow, dear? Come inside."

Danielle was very glad to sit
near Madame Beton's stove.
Before she knew it, Danielle
had told her everything.

When Danielle had finished, Madame Beton
took out her brushes.
    "May I watch you paint?" asked Danielle.
    "Of course. My studio is in here."

Danielle thought she was dreaming. "These look like my drawings.
How do you mix that red? Why does the smoke look real? Why . . ."

Madame Beton laughed. "So many questions! You know, I could use a bright assistant like you to wash brushes and sweep the floor . . . and maybe learn a little about painting."

"Here's your first week's pay,
in advance, of course—
that is, if you're interested."
    "Oh, yes!"

"I'll expect you here bright and early tomorrow morning—no sleeping late, now. Oh, and bring your drawings. I'd like to see them."

"I will!"

Danielle made one stop, then ran all the way home. "Papa! Papa!"
"Where have you been, Danielle? I've been so worried. But you're here now and safe. That's all that matters."
"And you, Papa, you're better. But I have wonderful news."

Danielle told Papa everything. "I start tomorrow!
But right now you have to close your eyes, no peeking."

"Now for the best part—look!"
"Pastries!"

There were not two more proud, happy, or hungry souls anywhere at that moment.

Papa sighed. "Like father, like daughter. Almost."